For Roger
xxx

Bradbury Press
An Affiliate of Macmillan, Inc.
866 Third Avenue, New York, NY 10022
Collier Macmillan Canada, Inc.
First produced 1989 in Great Britain by
Mathew Price Ltd, Somerset, England
First American Edition 1989

Printed and bound in Singapore

10 9 8 7 6 5 4 3 2 1

One Potato

Sue Porter

Bradbury Press

"Does anyone mind if I have the last, teeny, weeny potato?" asked Goat. Everyone minded. Everyone wanted it.

"Now let's be fair," said Cow. "Why don't we hold a competition for it?"

"Great!" said Goat, jumping onto his seat.
"Last one to stand on a chair loses."

"That's going to be difficult," snapped Cow, "since I don't have a chair."

"Such a pity," said Goat, who couldn't care less, "but somebody has to lose." Then, "The last one to stand on his head," he shouted, kicking his legs in the air.

"How can I do that?" hissed Goose.
"My neck's too wobbly."

"You've got a problem there," laughed Goat, as he disappeared up the hayloft ladder. "The last one in the hayloft loses."

"Don't start yet," puffed Pig. "I'm stuck."
"Too late old boy," said Goat. "You lose."

And with a great leap, he shouted,

"FIRST ONE DOWN WINS!"

"That's not fair," wailed Sheep, "I wasn't ready." And he kicked a load of hay over onto Goat.

"Perfectly fair," said Goat. "I win the potato."

Everyone looked at the plate.

But the potato had gone!

"Delicious," said a tiny voice.

"Now children, let's tell Goat what
we had for tea." And ten tiny mice
all squeaked together,

"ONE POTATO!"

THE END

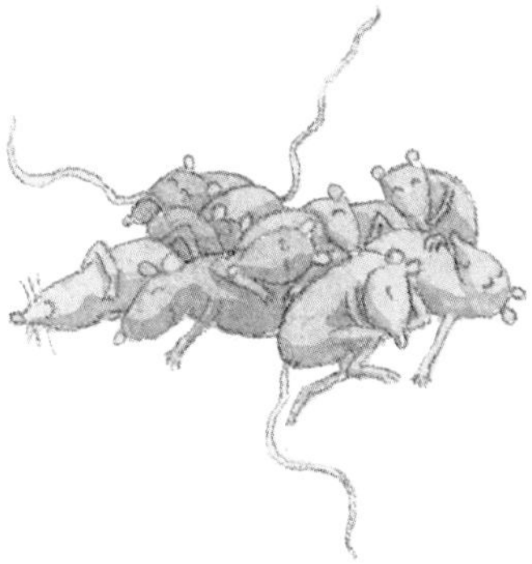